Shaun the Sheep™
Still Life
and
Washday

EGMONT
We bring stories to life

First published in Great Britain 2008 by Egmont UK Limited. 239 Kensington High Street, London W8 6SA

Based on original storylines by Richard Goleszowski, Robert Dudley and Trevor Ricketts.

© and ™ Aardman Animations Ltd. 2008. All rights reserved.
Shaun the Sheep (word mark) and the character 'Shaun the Sheep' © and ™ Aardman Animations Limited.
Based on a character created by Nick Park. Developed by Richard (Golly) Goleszowski with Alison Snowden and David Fine.

ISBN 978 1 4052 4168 7
1 3 5 7 9 10 8 6 4 2
Printed in Singapore

Still Life

It was a beautiful morning
on the farm. The sheep were
lounging in the sunshine,
Bitzer was tapping to the beats
on his personal stereo,
bmm-pah-chhh-pah
   bmm-pah-chhh-pah . . .
   All was well with the world.

The sound of jolly whistling phwit-phwittity-phwoo caught
Bitzer's attention and he gave a startled bark. The sheep began to
graze in a more sheeplike manner, as the Farmer strode into the field,
carrying a paintbox and a strange wooden stand. He peered around,
then looked happily over at the farmhouse.
He'd found the perfect
scene to paint!

Ohhhwaaa!

The Farmer propped up the stand and plonked a blank canvas on it. The wooden stand bent backwards with a crrrreeaaaak. Stupid easel! The Farmer huffed in annoyance as he propped it up again and reached for his paints.

Shlump. The canvas slid down the easel. "Ohhhwaaa!" the Farmer grumbled, nudging it back up.

The canvas slid down again. And again. And again. It finally landed with a smack on the ground. "Arrrrrgh!" The Farmer grunted and leaped on to the easel. He hammered and slammed, twisted and tweaked and stood the easel up again, fixed at last. Now he could get on with his painting!

slip-slap!

The Farmer pulled a beret out of the paintbox and fitted it smartly on his head. He thought he looked just like a proper artist, until Shaun and the sheep started smirking hehehehe at how silly he really looked. "Psst!" the Farmer shooed them away. He was a serious artist, not to be scoffed at!

The Farmer mixed his paints and began to slip-slap some colour on his canvas. Green for the grass, blue for the sky, white for the sheep . . . Wait a moment! Shaun had sneaked in front of the easel!

After all, what was a farm scene without sheep?

The Farmer shrugged and painted Shaun into the farm scene as a blob of white with a cheeky face, standing statue-still, next to a big, fat ball of wool . . . "Whoa!" The Farmer looked up in shock. Now Shirley had crept in to the scene! The Farmer began to paint her -- it took a lot of white paint.

Suddenly, the whole flock appeared in front of the Farmer, making him jump! "Arrrrgh!"

This wouldn't do. The Farmer whistled for Bitzer. Phwooo-wooo! Someone needed to get these sheep in order!

The Farmer told Bitzer where he wanted each sheep to appear in his painting, waving and pointing madly at the flock.

Bitzer obeyed with a grumpy sigh, shoving the sheep back and forth. Finally the Farmer seemed pleased with his new scene and gave Bitzer the thumbs-up.

Bitzer crept away to listen to his music again, keeping a lazy eye on the flock.

But Shaun and his fleecy friends soon got bored of posing for the Farmer's painting. Shirley stuck out her tongue with a loud "Luuuuurrrrrl!"

Then Shaun blew an ENORMOUS raspberry . . .

"Pppppthhhhhhhhhhtt!"

. . . making all the sheep bleat with laughter! "Baaaa!"

Baaaa!

Bitzer was not impressed. "Ruffff!" I've got my eye on you! he warned them with a growl. The sheep hung their heads in a sulk.

The Farmer squirted his tube of white paint to add a few clouds. But he had used it all up painting those sheep! The tube was empty! With a grumble, the Farmer threw off his beret and wandered back into the farmhouse to fetch some more.

Bitzer took the chance to sneak a peek at the Farmer's work of art.

"Ahhh!" he said, admiringly at first . . . then he realised there was something WRONG with this painting. Bitzer wasn't in it!

So Bitzer picked up the paintbrush and began to add his self-portrait – complete with blue woolly hat – at the very top of the scene.

Ahhhh!

tut-tut!

To his horror, the paint began to run down the canvas. Bitzer panicked. He rubbed, dabbed and scrubbed at the dribbling paint, making an ugly brown smudge!

Bitzer turned to see the flock tut-tutting at him. He'd ruined the picture!

Eagerly, Shaun came forward to save the painting.
Plonking the Farmer's beret on his woolly head, the little sheep
carefully dabbed at the canvas with the paintbrush, squinting
thoughtfully. Bitzer whimpered, covering his eyes. I can't watch!

Ta-da! Shaun stepped aside to show off his masterpiece —
a marvellous, peaceful country scene. "Beh!" he bleated proudly.

The sheep nodded in admiration, but each of them agreed that
the country scene was missing something.

SHEEP.

Ta-da!

Timmy's mum bustled forward. Timmy wanted a turn! She lifted the excited little sheep up, dipped him in the paint and **smooshed** his tiny face on to the canvas in shades of yellow, green and red!

Suddenly, the whole flock swayed towards the canvas in a big, woolly huddle to add to the artwork.

smoosh

sploosh

The sheep **splodged** and **splattered**, **smudged** and **splooshed**. Then they stepped back to admire their creation, a portrait of a smiling ewe they called 'The Mona Fleece-a'.

Shaun clapped his hooves together happily, as his fleecy friends picked up their paintbrushes again. This painting lark was fun!

But the sheep weren't stopping there.

As each sheep added to the picture, the paint flew everywhere, splattering the flock with amusing rainbow patches. Red, orange, yellow, blue . . .

Splat! Splat! Splat!

But in all the excitement, the sheep smacked into the canvas, smashing over the easel with a loud crrrrrack! The clumsy sheep landed in a multi-coloured heap.

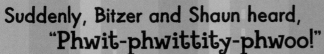

Suddenly, Bitzer and Shaun heard,
    "Phwit-phwittity-phwoo!"
The Farmer was coming out of the farmhouse, whistling and carrying a big pot of white paint, almost enough to paint a life-size portrait of Shirley. Quick! The sheepdog herded the paint-flecked flock out of the Farmer's sight.

The Farmer took one look at his painting and easel, lying sadly on the lawn, and wailed, "Ohhhhhhhhhhhhhhhh!"

It didn't take the Farmer long to work out who was to blame. The blobs of paint on each woolly coat gave the sheep away as the culprits!

stomp!

The Farmer stood in front of the sheepish sheep, including a shamefaced Shaun and a red-faced Timmy, and **stomped** his foot in fury. **Look what you've done!** He growled, rather like Bitzer!

baa-baa

The sheep baa-ed in embarrassment and huddled together. The Farmer stood his easel back up and took a good look. And then he wept.

The painting looked more like the work of a wacky modern artist than his own lovely landscape.
It was colourful . . . but was it art?
The Farmer didn't think so!

Grrraaaa-burrum-boom-grrraaa-burrum-boom....

The Farmer could hear loud rock music that for once wasn't coming from Bitzer's personal stereo.

A long, white limousine pulled up into the field, and the window opened, revealing the passenger, a famous rock star and well-known art collector.

The rock star pointed to the sheep-splattered masterpiece. It would look right at home in one of his mansions!

"Huh?" The Farmer pointed at what he thought was a MESS-terpiece.

A pile of bank notes appeared in the rock star's hand. Ker-ching! The Farmer – and the sheep for that matter – had never seen so much money!

SOLD! The Farmer handed over the painting to the rock star.

The rock star was overjoyed! The limousine drove away, wheels squealing in the mud, leaving the Farmer with his mouth wide open and a pile of bank notes in his hand.

Slowly but surely, the other sheep peered out from behind Shirley to find out what had happened.

The Farmer stared at the money, and back at the flock in a state of shock. But the shock soon wore off. Soon, he was hap-hap-happy!

In fact, he was over the moon! "Whoa-hoa-hoa-hoaaaa!"

The Farmer picked up little Timmy, with his bright-red-painted face, and gave the tiny sheep a great big KISS!

Mmmmwah!

He leaped and frolicked, skipped and cartwheeled across the lawn, dreaming of a shiny new Land-Rover and designer-label wellies. "Woo-hoooooo!"

Shaun and Bitzer, who had never seen the Farmer this happy and silly, looked at each other and shrugged.

But soon they, and the whole flock, were joining in the fun!

Beeeeeh!

Washday

One sunny morning, the sheep were **munching** their breakfast when the Farmer appeared, carrying a basket of clothes. Shaun perked up, feeling curious.

As the young sheep watched, the Farmer fiddled with a tall, thin thing that opened up to look like a weird, wiry tree. He hung clothes and sheets on its strings with little brown pegs.

Then the Farmer gave the wiry tree a nudge, and it spun round and round. **Whooooosh.**

Happy to have finished his chores for the day, the Farmer climbed into his Land-Rover and drove away. Shaun bleated excitedly. "Baaahhh!" This spinny thing looked like fun!

Plop!

Shaun and two of his chums scuttled over to the spinny thing and stood underneath, peering up.

Suddenly, a pair of attractive blue underpants dropped plop on the head of one of Shaun's pals, which the sheep thought very funny heeeheee! Shaun clambered on to the upturned laundry basket to peg the pants back on the spinny thing – but suddenly he slipped!

Hanging by a single hoof, the little sheep gripped on to the spinny thing for balance and found himself spinning as if he was on a crazy fairground ride!

Wheeeeeeeeeeeee!

bmm-papa-chhhh

Bitzer was supposed to keep an eye on the flock that morning, but instead he was enjoying himself, sitting in his comfy deckchair, reading his favourite soppy love story, gobbling pizza and listening listening to his stereo . . .

bmm-papa-chhhh-bmmm-papa-chhhh

He knew nothing of the chaos in the field . . .

Wheeeeeeeeeeeee!

Shaun's friends had leaped up to join him
on the spinny thing, which by now was
whizzing and whirling faster and faster!

Whoooooaaaaa!

"Whooooooaaaaa!" the sheep wailed, feeling dizzy. Sheets and shirts began to fly across the farmyard, over the heads of the crowd of sheep who were cheering on the daredevils.

One by one, the sheep lost their grip on the spinny thing, and zooomed through the air with bleats and shrieks.

BAAAAA!

They landed PLOP in a heap on the grass. Shaun was the last sheep left on the spinny thing. But suddenly, the brave little sheep lost his grip! He whooshed across the farmyard and landed headfirst in the pile of sheep, shirts and sheets. CRAAAASH!

CRAAAASH!

Urrrgh!

Bitzer was so busy with his pizza, his music and his book that he was unaware of the antics going on in the field. That is, until a sock landed splat on his pizza. As Bitzer greedily stuffed another slice into his mouth, he found himself with a mouthful of sock! Urrrgh!

Bitzer's eyes narrowed. The sheepdog was suspicious. Something was going on . . .

It was bound to be those sheep, up to no good again!

Sure enough, in the field,
the flock had gone crazy, holding
tugs of war with aprons and tablecloths,
and swinging through the trees on rope-swings
of jerseys and bed sheets! Washday was fun, fun, fun!

Wheeeeeeee!

Thweeeeee!

Bitzer blew on his whistle but the sheep were in a shambles. The sheepdog was surrounded by absolute chaos!

Watch out! Bitzer barked loudly as a shopping trolley with a duvet cover for a sail **zipped** towards him, driven by two rowdy sheep! Stop! Bitzer blew the whistle again but the sheep paid no attention.

Bitzer grabbed on to the handlebar and as the trolley crashed into the manure pile, he was thrown through the air, tangled in the duvet cover! He floated over the farmyard like a pink, flowery ghost. Wooooooooo!

Once he had landed, Bitzer untangled himself and glared at the flock. They'd gone too far this time!

The sheep looked ashamed. So much for putting his paws up while the Farmer was away! Bitzer stared at them, making them **wriggle** uncomfortably in their woolly jumpers. One by one they handed over the Farmer's laundry, which was now filthy again!

"Grrrr," growled Bitzer. He held up a bed sheet marked with muddy hoof-prints and sighed. There was only one solution . . .

Bitzer sat on the edge of the sheep dip, rubbing and scrubbing each item as clean as he could get it, and thinking mean thoughts about those sheep. This was not how he wanted to spend his day off, doing laundry! "Grufff!" he sulked.

Grufff!

Shhh!

Meanwhile, Shaun, being a clever sort of sheep, had discovered what was in the utility room. A big, white machine that had lots of buttons and dials on the front.

This was a washing machine!

Shhh!

40

While silly Bitzer scrubbed and soaked, the sheep had discovered a much quicker way to wash their whites!

The clever little sheep and his friends sneaked the laundry away from Bitzer Shhhh! and tossed it into the machine.

They also smuggled away the big box of powder with a soapy sheep on the front. Shaun realised it must go in with the washing, and tossed that into the machine too, along with a whole bubbly bottle of 'Soft 'n' Fleecy' fabric softener.

Splosh!

One of Shaun's helpful friends perched on top of the machine as Shaun pressed every button, twiddled the dial and then – hey presto! Beeeeep! The machine began to shake and shudder. Shaun's friend swayed from side to side and the machine wibbled and wobbled beneath her. This was fun!

Wibble wobble!

Shaun clambered on top of the machine next to his pal and after a quick wobble, he found his balance. As the clothes spun round and round, quicker and quicker beneath them, the two sheep juddered, jolted and danced a joyful jig!

Little did the shimmying sheep know that with all their dancing and prancing, the bubbly, soapy water was spilling out of the machine . . . and out under the utility room door. Uh-oh!

Suddenly . . .

KAAAAABLOOOOOOOOOOM!

The machine exploded!

The utility room door burst open and the laundry flew out and across the farmyard! Out came Shaun, balancing uncertainly on top of the silver drum bit of the washing machine like a clown, before landing

CRRRRASH!

in the Farmer's prize vegetable patch!

Bitzer gave a disapproving grrrrrrrowl.

Chuurnn

Luckily, the sheep had another idea. The cement mixer spun round and round. It would work like a washing machine — wouldn't it? It was worth a try. The laundry, the washing powder, complete with Bitzer's scrubbing board, were all thrown in. But the rough cement mixer was not meant for washing soft sheets and fluffy towels. It RIPPED the Farmer's clothes to shreds!

Bitzer groaned in despair as he poked his nose through a BIG hole in the Farmer's best T-shirt.

Shaun felt sorry for helping cause all this trouble. He thought extra hard, wracking his woolly little brain. Finding an answer to the problem of how to fix the Farmer's clothes was like trying to find a needle in a haystack . . .

. . . A needle! That was the answer!

Soon, the smart little sheep had come up with a Grand Plan.

Timmy and his mum used a needle to sew the Farmer's tattered towels and T-shirts together again. Then the sheep rolled Shirley back and forth over the clothes to press them flat, and Shaun loaded up the laundry basket.

Bitzer gave him a thumbs-up. Shaun had saved Washday!

Suddenly, there was a loud HONK HONK!

Bitzer gasped in panic. The Farmer was back! Bitzer blew his whistle, Peeeeeeep! Speedily, the last of the laundry was piled into the basket.

Oh!

Bitzer arrived at the Farmer's side, holding out his dried, ironed laundry. "Oh!" the Farmer exclaimed in delight.

PHEW! Bitzer collapsed on the grass, exhausted. What a morning!

Later that day, the Farmer, in his nice clean jeans and freshly washed woolly jumper, strode out of the farmhouse. Bitzer was impressed. The sheep had done well!

Suddenly, the Farmer turned on his welly heel to reveal patches where his clothes had torn, including one on his bottom!

Bitzer groaned, his head in his hands, as Shaun bleated cheekily beside him. Baaaa!